People Around Town

MEET THE FIREMAN

By Joyce Jeffries

 **Gareth Stevens**
Publishing

Please visit our website, www.garethstevens.com. For a free color catalog of all our high-quality books, call toll free 1-800-542-2595 or fax 1-877-542-2596.

Library of Congress Cataloging-in-Publication Data

Jeffries, Joyce.
  Meet the fireman / Joyce Jeffries.
      p. cm. — (People around town)
  Includes index.
  ISBN 978-1-4339-7329-1 (pbk.)
  ISBN 978-1-4339-7330-7 (6-pack)
  ISBN 978-1-4339-7328-4 (library binding)
  1. Fire fighters—Juvenile literature. I. Title.
  HD8039.F5J44 2013
  363.37—dc23

                                        2012007440

First Edition

Published in 2013 by
Gareth Stevens Publishing
111 East 14th Street, Suite 349
New York, NY 10003

Copyright © 2013 Gareth Stevens Publishing

Editor: Katie Kawa
Designer: Andrea Davison-Bartolotta

Photo credits: Cover, p. 13 Comstock/Thinkstock; p. 1 T-Design/Shutterstock.com; p. 5 © iStockphoto.com/ GMosher; p. 7 Stockbyte/Thinkstock; p. 9 Monkey Business Images/Shutterstock.com; p. 11 iStockphoto/ Thinkstock; pp. 15, 24 (boots) Wendy Kaveny Photography/Shutterstock.com; pp. 17, 24 (helmet) Nate A./ Shutterstock.com; p. 19 © iStockphoto.com/Joseph Abbott; pp. 21, 24 (hose) Ron Frank/Shutterstock.com; p. 23 Alan and Sandy Carey/Photodisc/Getty Images.

Printed in the United States of America

CPSIA compliance information: Batch #CS12GS: For further information contact Gareth Stevens, New York, New York at 1-800-542-2595.

Contents

A fireman puts out fires.

He works
in a fire station.

NO 1 TRUCK

EMERGENCY
FIRST
AID

"SECOND TO NONE"

His boss is the fire chief.

A loud noise tells him
when there is a fire.
It is called an alarm.

He puts on
special clothes.
These keep him safe
in a fire.

He puts boots
on his feet.
They are black
and yellow.

STEEL
MIDSOL
STEEL
MS

15

He wears a hard hat.
This is called a helmet.

He drives a fire truck.
The truck moves fast!

He uses a fire hose.
This puts a lot of water
on a fire.

One kind of fireman fights forest fires. He is called a smokejumper.

Words to Know

boots

helmet

hose

Index